NANCY CLANCY
Secret Admirer

NANCY CLANCY

Secret Admirer

WRITTEN BY
Jane O'Connor

ILLUSTRATIONS BY
Robin Preiss Glasser

SCHOLASTIC INC.

ISBN 978-0-545-85504-4

12 11 10 9 8 7 6 5 4 3 2 1   15 16 17 18 19 20/0

Printed in the U.S.A.   40

First Scholastic printing, March 2015

Typography by Jeanne L. Hogle

To Doug Stewart,
from your out-in-the-open admirer
—J.O'C.

For Garrett, Jessie's fiancé,
which is a fancy word for *not*-so-secret admirer
—R.P.G.

CONTENTS

CHAPTER 1

BEATING HEARTS

"On your marks, get set . . ."

Mr. Dudeny paused for a second. "Go!"

Right away Nancy started counting. *One, two, three.* The tips of her fingers were pressed against her neck.

Four, five, six, seven, eight.

1

All the kids in room 3D were counting how many times their hearts beat in a minute. This was called taking your pulse.

Twenty, twenty-one, twenty-two.

Mr. Dudeny was watching the seconds go by on the wall clock.

Forty-nine, fifty, fifty-one.

Human Heart

For the past week, room 3D had been learning about the heart. Real hearts didn't look anything like the hearts that Nancy drew.

Seventy-two, seventy-three.

Real hearts weren't even red like the ones on Valentine's Day cards.

Eighty-five, eighty-six.

Nancy closed her eyes and tried to feel all the blood that her heart was pumping around inside her. But she couldn't feel anything. It was kind of hard to believe that she really had a heart like the one on the poster in her classroom.

"Okaaaaaay—stop!"

"My heart beat ninety times," Bree said.

"I think I got eighty-nine," Nancy said.

Robert got eighty-seven. Olivia got ninety-three.

"Me too," said Nola.

"Ha! My heart beat the fastest!" Grace shouted. "I got ninety-seven."

"This wasn't a race, Grace," Mr. Dudeny said. "And nobody's heart beats at the same rate all the time." Then he turned to Clara. "Is something the matter?"

"My heart only beat seven times!" she said.

Lionel jumped up. "Call an ambulance! This is a medical emergency!"

"Dude, sit down and stop acting silly."

Just then the bell rang. Everybody grabbed their backpacks and headed for the door. Everybody except Clara.

"Bye, Mr. Dude. See you Monday," Nancy called.

Mr. Dude waved. He was standing over Clara's desk. Nancy heard him saying, "Don't be upset. You are *not* having a heart attack. Your heart is strong and healthy." Then he took Clara's fingers and helped her take her pulse again.

Mr. Dude was the best teacher ever. Not only was he smart and funny, he was nice, too. No, he was much better than nice: He was kindhearted!

As she walked home with Bree, Nancy thought more about that word— "kindhearted."

"We say people are kindhearted. But a heart can't really be kind, can it?" she asked.

"I guess not." Bree was busy sucking on a grape Ring Pop.

"And we call mean people heartless," Nancy went on. "Like they don't have a heart. But everybody has one."

Bree nodded. Nancy could tell that she wasn't really interested. To Nancy, however, it was important. If the heart was just some muscle, like Mr. Dudeny said, then what made people fall in love?

CHAPTER 2

GUITAR HERO

Andy arrived soon after Nancy got home. He high-fived her, then slung his guitar off his shoulder and tossed his Red Sox cap on the couch. He wore his baseball cap everywhere. Nancy thought he looked much cuter without it.

This was Nancy's sixth guitar lesson.

Andy was teaching her an old rock song. It was called "Wild Thing."

"What's up, JoJo?" he asked Nancy's little sister. Only the way he said it was like this: "Wazzup." That was how teenagers talked. Then Andy picked JoJo up and twirled her around and around. It looked like she was flying.

"Again!" JoJo said.

Nancy's mom came in. "Oh, no, missy! We have to leave Andy and Nancy alone."

"So?" Andy asked as he handed JoJo over to Mom. "Has my best student been practicing?"

Nancy giggled. Of course she was Andy's best student. She was Andy's *only* student. Her mom had answered an ad he had put up on the bulletin board at the supermarket.

Nancy snapped open
her guitar case. Her
guitar was turquoise with
little tuning knobs made of
imitation ivory. It was Nancy's
most prized possession.
Holding the guitar neck
with her left hand, Nancy
began strumming with
her pick. It was imita-
tion ivory too. As she did,
she switched chords from A to D to E major
and back to A.

"Yesss! What I'm hearing is rock . . .
and . . . roll!" Andy strapped on his guitar
and started playing along with Nancy.

"Wild thing!" Andy sang. "You make my

heart sing! You make everything . . ." Andy looked over at Nancy.

"Groovy!" She sang in a low, growly voice the way Andy did.

For the next forty-five minutes Nancy kept playing. Andy showed her how to play a G chord and a C chord. Andy was a superb guitar player. And he was almost a celebrity. His band played at sweet-sixteen parties and bar mitzvahs.

"You were totally rockin' the joint today!"  he told her afterward. "With the five chords you know now, you can play lots of songs."

They were drinking lemonade in the kitchen. JoJo was sitting on Andy's lap. She was holding his glass.

"Andy, what are you doing for Valentine's Day?" Nancy asked.

Andy shrugged. "No plans." Then he turned to JoJo and shouted, "More lemonade!"

JoJo shook her head no.

"I want lemonade! Now!" It was a game

JoJo had made up. Andy had to act like a bratty little kid. He had to remember to say please before JoJo gave him lemonade. It was a dumb game. But JoJo thought it was hilarious.

"I think you should serenade your girl-friend outside her window." Serenade meant singing love songs to someone. It was very romantic.

"What girlfriend?" Andy asked.

"Margaret! Your girlfriend, Margaret. Remember?" Nancy had asked a million questions about Margaret. Andy's girl-friend had long brown hair, green eyes, and was almost seventeen.

"Oh, we broke up," Andy said. He didn't sound upset. But Nancy was.

"Why?"

"She said we didn't spend enough time together. I thought we spent *way* too much time together."

Nancy thought about that. "Margaret wasn't the right girl for you," she said with certainty. She finished her lemonade. "When you find that special someone, you'll never want to part."

"If you say so." Andy put JoJo down. He went and got his baseball cap and his guitar. "So? Next week, same time, same place!"

Nancy waved as he drove off in his pickup truck. She hoped Andy found the love of his life soon. Valentine's Day was only a week away!

15

CHAPTER 3

THE BEST BABYSITTER IN THE UNIVERSE

On Saturday night, as soon as Bree's little brother, Freddy, was asleep, Nancy and Bree had Annie all to themselves.

Annie was the best babysitter in the universe. Annie let Nancy and Bree style her hair. (It was so long she could sit on it!)

Annie gave almost perfect manicures—the polish never smooshed!—and Annie knew all the words to loads of songs.

Right now they were all dancing to a hip-hop song. Annie had awesome moves.

"Ooh! That was superb!" Nancy said. "Do it again!"

Annie spun around, stopped short, and did a hop and a kick while her arms moved up and down like a robot's.

When the song was over, they all collapsed on the sofa. Nancy was perspiring. "Perspiring" sounded more grown-up than "sweating." She was also breathing hard.

"I bet my heart is beating five hundred times a minute!" Nancy said.

"No. That's impossible," Bree said. Then she told Annie what they had learned about the heart. "Hummingbirds' hearts beat about a thousand times a minute. But not human-being hearts."

"I don't think that Nancy was being literal," Annie said to Bree. She explained that literal meant sticking to facts. That was another great thing about Annie. She knew a ton of fancy words.

At nine thirty, Annie said, "It's your bedtime. And I have to start studying for my French test."

Bree pooched out her lips. "But we didn't get to look through your fashion magazines."

"Okay, we can. But after your teeth are brushed and you're both in your pj's."

"Deal!" Nancy and Bree said together.

A few minutes later, the trundle under Bree's bed had been pulled out. Annie sat between Bree and Nancy. Slowly, they leafed through every page of *Glamour Girl,* deciding which outfits were chic. Annie said chic was French for cool. Annie said it like this: "sheek."

On page 156 was a quiz: "Is Your Boyfriend Right for You?" There was a photo of a girl staring at a boy. Over his head was a big question mark.

"Ooh! Can we give you the quiz?" Bree asked. "Then you'll know if Dan is right for you." Dan was Annie's boyfriend.

"I don't need to take the quiz. I already know the answer," Annie said.

"Oh, that's so romantic!" Nancy clasped her hands together. "You're madly in love with Dan!"

But Annie was shaking her head. "No. That's not what I meant. Dan and I broke up. He definitely wasn't right for me."

"What went wrong?" Bree asked. "You loved his dimples and his laugh. Remember?"

"Yeah, I guess." Annie closed the magazine. "Maybe the problem was that he was too nice."

Being nice was a problem? Nancy said, "I don't understand."

Annie shut the magazine. "Oh, whatever I wanted to do was always fine with him. Whatever I said, he agreed with. It got boring."

Then Annie climbed over Nancy and blew the girls a kiss. As she turned off the light she said, "I have a date with my French book. So *bonne nuit!*"

In French that meant good night. Annie said it like this: "bun new-wee."

"I wish Annie had a real date tonight," Nancy whispered in the dark.

"Then she couldn't have come to baby-sit," Bree pointed out.

Yes. That was true. But Bree was being too—what was that word Annie had used? Too literal.

CHAPTER 4

HEARTS AND MORE HEARTS

The next morning, Bree and Nancy were in their clubhouse. It was in Nancy's backyard. They had allowed JoJo and Freddy to come too.

The sign outside said SLEUTH HEADQUARTERS. A sleuth was a detective. And both Nancy and Bree were superb sleuths. The file for their first case was inside a bright pink folder. It told all about catching the thief who had stolen Mr. Dudeny's big blue marble.

Nancy had bought a package of pink folders for all the cases they were going to solve. However, the other folders were still empty. Nobody seemed to be committing crimes lately. So Nancy and Bree were at Sleuth Headquarters doing homework.

Doing homework was Bree's idea. Nancy didn't see the point. Their Appreciation Hearts didn't have to be handed in until Friday.

Mr. Dudeny thought that third graders were too grown-up—"mature" was what he said—to give Valentine's Day cards to one another. Instead, everyone was making Appreciation Hearts. Appreciating someone meant liking them.

"Dudes, think of a reason why you appreciate each person in 3D," Mr. Dude had said. Then he passed out envelopes. Inside each were lots of paper hearts, along with a list of the kids in the class.

"What about kids we don't like? Can we say why we unappreciate them?" Grace asked.

"I won't bother answering that question," was all Mr. Dudeny said.

Grace. Finding something good to say about Grace was going to be a challenge.

That meant it was going to be very, very, very, very hard. Nancy lay on her back, staring up at the butterfly mobile in the clubhouse. No matter how hard she blew, it didn't move.

Already Bree had a stack of hearts finished. Nancy had only done two. For Yoko, she had written, *I appreciate Yoko because she taught me cat's cradle.* For Lionel she had written, *I appreciate Lionel because he is humorous and artistic.*

"This heart is for Andy." JoJo held up a scribble. "I love Andy." JoJo said she was going to make a heart for everybody she loved.

"Me too." Freddy put down the space guy he had been playing with. "One for Mama, one for Daddy, one for Nana." He went on making scribble hearts. "And one for Annie. When I go to bed, Annie sings to me," he told JoJo. "I love her."

All at once, Nancy sat up. She could feel an idea taking root in her mind. Andy didn't have a girlfriend. Annie didn't have a boyfriend. "Bree!" she said excitedly.

Bree didn't answer. She was checking over the class list. "Mmmm. Let's see. Whose name is next?"

Andy and Annie. Their names went together like two puzzle pieces.

Annie and Andy. It sounded like the title of a song!

Ooh la la! Nancy's idea kept growing. She could almost feel it blooming into a flower. Not just any flower, but a beautiful red rose for Valentine's Day.

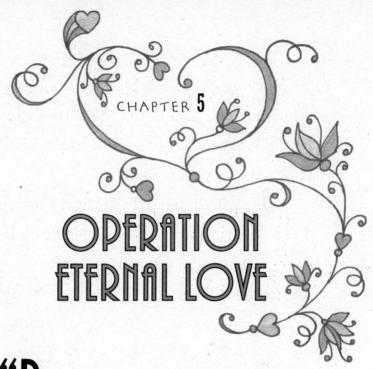

CHAPTER **5**

OPERATION ETERNAL LOVE

"**B**ree, stop doing homework and listen to me. Let's make Andy and Annie fall in love!"

Bree frowned as she let Nancy's words sink in. For a moment Nancy was worried. Maybe Bree thought this was a crazy idea. But a second later, Bree sprang from the beanbag chair. She started shouting, "Yes! Yes! Yes!" and doing the little dance she did whenever she made a soccer goal. "That's the best idea ever!"

Nancy smiled modestly and said *merci*. "You think we can make them fall in love before Valentine's Day?" she asked once Bree calmed down.

"Or what about right *on* Valentine's Day!"

"Ooh. That's way better," Nancy said.

Bree had a dreamy look on her face. "Years from now, Annie and Andy will tell their kids about meeting on Valentine's Day. How they fell in love the minute they gazed into each other's eyes."

"Andy and Annie. Don't you love saying it?" Nancy imagined double hearts with

their names written in swirly letters.

"So?" Bree flopped back down in the beanbag chair. "How will we get them to meet?"

Nancy frowned. "I haven't exactly worked that part out yet."

"We need a plan."

"Yes!" Nancy said. "We can call it Operation Eternal Love." Eternal love meant loving someone forever, to infinity.

"Fine." Bree bit her lower lip. "What if I call Annie, or you could call Andy and say, 'Guess what! I know the perfect person for you. You're definitely going to fall in love. So call this number . . .'" Bree stopped. "No, that'll never work."

"Yeah, Andy's not going to call some girl because I said so. We need to arrange for them to meet someplace," Nancy said. "Only they can't know we're behind it."

Bree wrinkled her nose. "That's going to be hard."

"We'll think of something," Nancy assured her. Then she got the package of pink folders, and on the front of one she wrote *Operation Eternal Love* in big purple letters.

Sure enough, that very afternoon Nancy stumbled upon a plan.

Nancy was helping Dad with the grocery shopping. Before getting in line to check out, they stopped at the greeting card aisle. Her dad needed to pick out some Valentine's Day cards.

"Hey! This is a good one to give Mom!" He showed Nancy a card. There was a photo of a gorilla in a top hat and it said "I go ape for you!"

"No, Dad! All wrong! Nothing humorous!"

Instead Nancy found a card with a puffy
red satin heart on the front. It said "For my
beloved wife, my heart belongs to you and

only you." Then her eyes fell on another card. Ooh la la! The card was silver, and in silver glitter it said "From your secret admirer." Inside was a love poem.

"Get this one, Dad."

On the way home, Nancy asked, "What exactly *is* a secret admirer, Dad?"

"Hmmm. How can I explain it? It's when you love somebody but you don't tell them. Not right away. Instead, you leave presents—like flowers or poems—and write 'This is from your secret admirer.'"

That was just about the most romantic thing Nancy had ever heard!

"Were you Mom's secret admirer?" Nancy asked at home, while they were putting away groceries. "Did you worship her from afar?"

Her mom came into the kitchen and heard Nancy.

"Worship me from afar?" Mom looked at Dad and laughed. "No, sweetie. Your father didn't know I existed, even though he sat right next to me in a history class."

"Is that true, Dad?"

"If your mother says so."

Mom helped put away cartons of ice cream and packages of meat. "Then right before exam time, suddenly Dad started to notice me."

"Ooh la la! He realized you were the

girl of his dreams!"

Mom shut the freezer door. "He realized he needed help studying. Serious help."

"Were you a bad student, Dad?"

"Uh, I was more what you might call a student of life."

Nancy turned from her dad to her mom. "What does that mean?"

Nancy's mother was smiling. "It means that in college your father never missed a party and spent way too much time playing Hacky Sack."

"Team captain," her dad said proudly. "Undefeated our final season. Let's not forget that!"

"Thanks to me, you passed that history exam."

"And the rest is history!" Dad said. He

wrapped his arms around Nancy's mom and kissed her. "I never looked at another girl!"

Nancy went upstairs to her room, flopped on her bed, and pondered. Yes, her parents had found true love. But it wasn't a very romantic story. It would have been so much better if her dad had been secretly admiring her mother and then finally declared his love.

That was definitely the way Annie and Andy had to fall in love, Nancy decided. There was only one problem. How could Andy be Annie's secret admirer when he didn't even know her?

CHAPTER **6**

A PRIVATE CONVERSATION

B ree came up with the answer during recess on Monday. It was while she was hanging upside down on the jungle gym. Bree claimed to do her best thinking upside down. "All the blood from my heart goes straight to my brain," she said, "and makes it work better."

That didn't sound scientific. But maybe it was true. Because Bree's plan was superb. She swung right side up and explained it to Nancy.

"Every day we'll leave something for Annie at her front door. Like candy. Or a rose. And each time the note will say 'From your secret admirer.'"

Nancy was straddling a bar on the jungle gym. Hanging upside down didn't make her any smarter. It just made her dizzy. "Oh! So we're pretending to be Andy!"

"Who's Andy?" Grace asked. She was swinging from a rung above Bree and Nancy.

"This is a private conversation," Bree informed Grace.

Nancy inched closer to Bree. "Let's leave

a poem for Annie, too. A love poem!" she
whispered.

Grace climbed down a rung. "Have you
done an Appreciation Heart about me yet?"

"No," Bree said.

Nancy just shook her head. She'd finished a couple more hearts last night. But she still had a lot to go.

"I did both of yours." Then in a singsong voice, Grace said, "Want me to tell what I wrote?"

Secretly Nancy did. But right away, Bree shook her head. "No. Mr. D said it's supposed to be a surprise." Bree was much stricter about rules than Nancy.

A moment later, Mr. Dudeny called out that recess was over. That meant that Bree and Nancy had to wait until lunchtime to plan out more of Operation Eternal Love.

♥ ♥ ♥

Bree and Nancy sat at their usual table under a poster about the four food groups.

"What if we drop clues for Annie?" Bree said as she unfolded a napkin and spread it carefully on top of her tray.

"Clues?" Nancy watched Bree arrange her sandwich, milk box, apple slices, and bag of trail mix on the tray. Bree was very neat about lunch.

"Like in the first love note we say, 'My first name starts with an 'A,' just like yours,'" Bree explained. "It'll make it even more mysterious."

"Oh!" This was such a superb idea. Nancy wished she had thought of it herself. "And in another one, we say, 'I play guitar. Soon I will serenade you, my darling!'"

Bree giggled. "That's really good!"

Yoko and Clara came and sat at their table.

"Let's tell them! Please, please!" Nancy

begged Bree. Operation Eternal Love was too good to keep just to themselves.

"Tell us what?" Clara asked.

As soon as Clara and Yoko locked their lips and threw away the key, Nancy said, "We're going to make two teenagers fall in love!"

"Wow! It's like something out of a movie!" Yoko said once she heard their plan.

"I know!" said Nancy. It *was* like a movie. In the last scene, Annie and Andy would be walking down a street holding hands. . . . No, no. They wouldn't be on a street. They'd be on a beach holding hands. At sunset. Then suddenly the words "The End" would pop up over their heads.

"I don't understand." Clara had pulled

apart an Oreo cookie and was licking off the filling. "How can they fall in love if they don't know each other?"

"Simple." Nancy held up the granola bar in her lunch box to see if anybody wanted it. Nobody did. "They are going to meet on Valentine's Day."

"How?" Clara wanted to know. "Where?"

"Um, we're still planning that part," Bree said.

"You only have till Friday," Yoko pointed out.

That was true. Time was of the essence. That was something Mr. Dudeny often said. It meant there wasn't a minute to waste.

♥ ♥ ♥

After school, Nancy and Bree set Operation Eternal Love into motion. They rode over to Annie's house. No car was in the driveway. And nobody was out walking a dog.

"It looks like the coast is clear!" Nancy said. A shiver of excitement wiggled through her. This was almost like sleuthing! They parked their bikes a few houses down from Annie's. Then Nancy grabbed the love note and the granola bar from her bike basket. Nancy wished they had a fancy box of candy, the kind where each piece sat in a little pleated paper cup. But Bree kept insisting, "It's the thought that counts."

Lickety-split they dashed down to

Annie's house. As they reached the porch, a dog inside started yapping like mad. They left the note and granola bar right by the front door. Then they made a quick getaway.

On the ride back home, Nancy imagined the look on Annie's face when she read the note. It was written on a rose-pink index card and said:

Annie, my sweetheart, you hold the key to my heart.
—From your secret admirer

Hint #1: My name starts with an "A," just like yours.

At the bottom, in silver gel-pen ink, Nancy had drawn a fancy key. Bree had written all the words because her script looked more grown-up than Nancy's.

As Nancy turned the corner onto their street, she was filled with a sense of satisfaction. Andy and Annie were one step closer to falling in love!

CHAPTER 7

WHEN IT RAINS, IT POURS

Step two did not go as smoothly. First it started pouring almost the minute school let out. Nancy and Bree had to run the whole way home.

Nancy was out of breath by the time they reached Bree's house. She flung herself on the sofa, panting.

Bree pointed to a vase on the hall table. "There are the roses."

"Oh." Nancy was disappointed. "They look so droopy."

"What do you expect? My mom's birthday was last week." Nancy went over and picked out the ones that still had most of their petals.

"I don't know," Bree said, watching Nancy. "Mom might get mad."

"Don't be silly." Nancy tied her hair ribbon around the roses. "Your mom has plenty left. They're going to get tossed soon anyway."

"I guess." Bree didn't look convinced.

Then Nancy raced home and brought back the Valentine's Day card that her dad had bought. "Here. Read this," she said, handing Bree the silver secret admirer card.

Bree read it aloud:

"No other eyes shine like your eyes.
They sparkle like stars in the night skies.
And your smile is like the morning sun,
Spreading warmth on everyone.
It's you I'm always thinking of.
To you I pledge eternal love."

"Doesn't that say it all?" Nancy smiled and sighed. "I'll get a pink index card so you can write it down."

"Oh, no! No way!" Bree shoved the card back at Nancy. "That's copying!"

Nancy sighed. "Okay, okay."

Together they came up with another
love poem.

Roses are red,
Violets are blue.
My eternal love is all
Pledged to you.

"This isn't nearly as good," Nancy
grumbled.

Bree said exactly what Nancy knew
she would say: "It's the thought that
counts."

Nancy returned Dad's valentine, then
got her raincoat, helmet, and bike. Bik-
ing to Annie's in the rain was no fun. By

the time they got there, Bree and Nancy
were soaking wet.

Once again, the house looked deserted,
which meant nobody was home.

They ran up the porch steps.

Once again, the dog started yipping.

"Aw, some of the ink ran," Bree said as they put the card and flowers on the mat by the front door. "It looks like it says 'For Amie.'"

The roses had also lost more petals.

"Nancy? Nancy Clancy?" they suddenly heard someone shouting.

Nancy and Bree spun around.

A truck had pulled to a stop right in front of Annie's house. It was Andy's old pickup truck. Inside it was Andy!

CHAPTER 8

A CLOSE CALL

"**H**ey!" Andy rolled down the window. "I thought it was you!"

Nancy's brain froze. She gulped. "H-hi, Andy!"

"That's Andy?" Bree whispered. When Nancy nodded, Bree let out a squeak like a mouse. "What do we say?"

Nancy didn't know. Her brain was still frozen.

"What are you doing over here?" Andy asked. Then he pointed to their bikes. "Those yours?"

"Um, yeah. We were—uh, we were riding our bikes." Nancy licked her lips and blinked. "Then it started raining really hard. So . . . so we ducked under this porch for a minute." The words just seemed to pop out of her mouth all on their own. But they made sense. Kind of. "I have no idea who lives here," she added.

"Come on. I'll give you girls a ride home."

Oh no! Andy was getting out of the truck. What if Annie came home now? It would mess up everything!

Andy picked up both bikes and put

them in the back of the truck. Nancy and Bree scrambled into the front seat. Nancy peered down the street. So far, there was no sign of Annie.

Before Andy started the engine, he turned to Nancy. "Aren't you going to introduce me to your friend?"

"Sorry. This is Bree," Nancy said hurriedly.

"Hi." Bree smiled a nervous smile. Too many of her teeth were showing.

"Okay, away we go." Andy took out his key and started the engine. At least, he tried to. Each time, the

truck made a funny noise.

"This happens all the time," he said. "It'll just take a second to fix. Don't look so worried, Nancy."

Worried? Nancy wasn't worried. She was frazzled. She was frantic! She was panic-stricken! Everything was going wrong! While Andy got under the hood of his truck, Nancy and Bree scrunched way down in front so maybe Annie wouldn't see them if she came by.

Hurry, Andy. Hurry, Andy! Nancy was shouting in her head. Nancy was almost 100 percent positive that she and Bree could send thoughts to each other. But they were best friends. Andy was only her guitar teacher.

At last Andy returned and—ooh la la!—this time the engine sprang to life. The truck took off down the street. At the corner, a red station wagon was waiting to make a turn.

"That's Annie's car!" Bree whispered to Nancy.

They had gotten away in the nick of time!

"Merci beaucoup!" Nancy said to Andy when they reached her house. She and Bree hopped down from the truck. "See you Friday. Same time. Same place."

"'Fraid not," Andy said as he got their bikes down. "I need to call your mom. I got a gig late Friday afternoon." Andy was going to play guitar at the Candy Café for some little kid's birthday party.

"Oh! JoJo's going to that party!" Nancy exclaimed.

"So is Freddy—he's my little brother," Bree added.

"Maybe we can switch your guitar lesson to Saturday." Andy got back in the truck, tipped his baseball cap to Bree and Nancy, and drove off.

"Talk about a close call!" Nancy said once Andy's truck was out of sight.

Bree's hand was pressed against her chest. "My heart is pounding so hard. I have to sit down."

In the kitchen, Nancy poured two big glasses of apple juice. While she gulped

70

hers down, Nancy thought about what Andy had just told them. "Bree, maybe running into Andy was a stroke of luck."

"It was?"

"Think about it!" Nancy paused. "Now we know where Andy and Annie can meet Friday!"

A smile began to break out on Bree's face. She jumped up and started doing her little victory dance. "Yessss! The Candy Café!"

The birthday party invitation was on the fridge. The party ended at five o'clock.

"They always have cake at the end,"

Bree said. "Andy's gig will be over right before then."

Nancy nodded. "So around a quarter to five is when Annie has to show up. Oh, Bree, this is all working out!"

Bree said, "We can go to the Candy Café when it's time to pick up JoJo and Freddy." A dreamy look came over her face. "We can spy on Annie and Andy and watch them fall in love!"

Nancy poured herself more juice. "Maybe it wasn't just luck that Andy drove by!" she said, squinting her eyes in deep thought. "Of all the streets in town, why did Andy pick Annie's street to drive down? Maybe he was drawn to her house like a magnet."

"Ooooh." Bree sat back and let this sink in. "It's like their love is meant to be!"

"Exactly!" Then Nancy clinked her glass against Bree's and they both said at the same time, "To eternal love!"

CHAPTER **9**

THE MESSENGER

On Wednesday, the letter that Nancy and Bree left on Annie's porch said:

My darling,

I cannot keep my eternal love a secret any longer. Please meet me on Friday at the Candy Café. Be there at twilight.

(That is 4:45.) I am tall, dark, and handsome. I will be wearing a Red Sox baseball cap.

Check one of the boxes below:

❏ *YES, I will be there.*

❏ *NO, I am not coming.*

Leave your answer at the bench by the swings at the playground.

P.S. Maybe use some tape so it won't blow away.

♥ ♥ ♥

Thursday was the longest school day ever. Nancy couldn't wait until three o'clock when she and Bree could bike to the playground. What if Annie's answer was no? Then all their hard work would have been a waste. It was too heartbreaking to think about!

Even during creative writing, Nancy's mind kept wandering. All she did was fill her paper with doodles. Little hearts. Big hearts. Hearts with frills around the edges. Inside each one were two script "A"s.

"Daydreaming, Nancy?"

Nancy looked up. "Yes. Sorry, Mr. D."

"I'm eager to find out what Lucette is up to next."

Lucette Fromage was a nine-year-old girl that Nancy had made up. In the last story, Lucette Fromage had caught a gang of jewel thieves. Now Lucette was trying to reunite a prince and the poor village girl he loved. One reason why Mr. D liked Nancy's stories was that she used vivid, interesting words, like "reunite," which meant get back together.

Mr. Dude said, "Sometimes a writer needs to daydream. Writers can get superb ideas from daydreaming."

Nancy smiled. She loved Mr. D so much. Not in an eternal-love kind of way. But because he was so wise and understanding.

At last, the minute hand crept up to the twelve and the hour hand reached the three. The bell on the wall in their classroom rang.

School was out!

Nancy and Bree jumped from their seats, raced down the hall, and burst outside. While they were stashing stuff in their bike baskets, Grace came over to them.

"Bree, your mom is parked around the corner. She told me to tell you that she's driving you and Nancy home."

"What?!" Bree and Nancy cried. "Why?"

Grace shrugged. "How should I know?"

Bree turned to Nancy. "This ruins everything."

"Ruins what?" Grace asked eagerly. "Ruins what?" she repeated, tagging along as they wheeled their bikes over to Bree's mother's car.

"Why can't we bike home?" Bree asked her mom. "We don't need you to drive us."

It turned out that Nancy's mom was working late. Bree's mom was picking up JoJo and Freddy from preschool and then doing some errands. "I don't want you girls staying in the house alone. I've got the trunk open. Put your bikes in back and jump in." Bree's mom had a

81

"don't argue" look on her face. Still, Bree gave it a try.

"We have to bike over to the playground," Bree said. "It's very important. Pleeeeeeeease." She strung the word out forever.

It didn't work.

"What's so important?" Grace wanted to know. "Why do you have to go to the playground?"

"None of . . ." Nancy was starting to say "None of your beeswax." Then she remembered something. Grace lived across the street from the playground.

"Grace, will you do something for us?" Nancy asked.

"Maybe. But not for free. You'll have to pay me back. Deal?"

Nancy rolled her eyes, then nodded. "Deal."

"Nancy, hurry up," Bree's mother called. Bree was already in the backseat, pouting.

Quickly Nancy told Grace what she had to do.

"Call right after!" Nancy said as she buckled up the seat belt. "I'll be at Bree's."

CHAPTER 10

SWEET SUCCESS

Every time the phone rang, Nancy and Bree jumped.

At last Bree's mom said, "Bree, Nancy. It's Grace on the phone."

Bree got right down to business. "Did you find the note, Grace?"

"Yes."

"Well, does it say yes or no?" Nancy asked. It was hard sharing one phone.

"First you have to tell me what going's on."

Nancy groaned. So did Bree. But they told Grace.

"That's, like, the stupidest thing I've ever heard," Grace told them.

Nancy was about to say there was no such word as "stupidest." Instead she shouted, "Just tell us what Annie said!"

"She said no, she isn't coming!"

Bree and Nancy looked at each other. Nancy's lips trembled. Bree already had tears in her eyes.

"Ha! I'm only kidding!" Grace was laughing into the phone. "The box for *yes* is checked."

"You'd better not be kidding this time, Grace!" Bree said.

"I'll bring it to school tomorrow. You can see for yourself. And here's what you have to do to pay me back."

A minute later they hung up.

Nancy was thrilled. Andy and Annie

were meeting tomorrow! It wasn't just a plan anymore. It was really happening. She didn't even mind having Grace sit at their table at lunch for two weeks. Well, she minded, but it was worth it.

♥ ♥ ♥

At home later, Nancy practiced playing guitar. Then she finished up the last of her Appreciation Hearts. They had to be handed in tomorrow. She did Nola's and Richard's and Isabel's. In a little while there were checks by everyone's names on the class list. Everyone except Grace's. Nancy felt bad that it was so hard to find a reason to like Grace.

"Nancy. The phone is for you," Nancy heard her mom calling.

When she picked it up, she heard

Grace's voice.

"Uh, Nancy? Listen, you and Bree don't have to pay me back. The favor is for free."

What? Nancy almost asked Grace why she was being nice. Instead, she said, "*Merci*, Grace. I truly appreciate it and— and look. I guess you can still sit with us."

Nancy got off the phone. Suddenly she knew exactly what to write on Grace's heart: *I appreciate Grace because she did a favor for me.* Then Nancy put extra glitter on Grace's heart.

Just then, the bell on the Top-Secret Special Delivery mailbox started ringing.

That meant Bree was sending a message. The basket hung from a rope between their bedroom windows.

Nancy reached for the note. It was not written in code. That had to mean Bree was in a super rush to get in touch.

When she read it, Nancy understood.

The note in the basket said "Annie's baby-sitting. Come over *toute de suite!*" *Toute de suite* meant right away in French. You say it like this: "toot-deh-sweet."

Since all of Nancy's homework was done, her mom said okay.

"Guess what! Annie has a secret admirer!" Bree said the second Nancy walked in the door. Bree was hopping all around and acting excited. "Wait till you hear!"

Nancy had never realized what a good

actress Bree was. So Nancy tried to act really surprised too. "A secret admirer? Wow!" Nancy let her jaw drop open.

Annie was helping Freddy build a Lego rocket ship. "Yes! I'm meeting him tomorrow. At the Candy Café."

"Do you have any idea who it is?" Nancy asked Annie.

"Not really. He's tall, dark, and handsome and plays guitar."

"He left flowers for Annie. Roses!" Bree really sounded as if this were news to her.

"Ooh la la! That's so romantic. What did the love poem say?"

Annie looked up from the floor. "Who said anything about a love poem?"

Whoopsy! Bad slip! "Um—it's like a rule," Nancy stammered. "Secret admirers always leave a love poem."

Quickly Bree switched the subject. "Annie, how will you wear your hair tomorrow?" Then, when Annie took Freddy up to bed, Bree glared and said, "I can't believe it. You nearly blew the whole thing!"

"I'm so sorry! It just slipped out. You think she suspects?"

"No. But watch what you say!" Bree glanced at the stairs. "Shh. I hear Annie coming."

Freddy was asleep, so Bree and Nancy had Annie all to themselves now. First they took turns brushing Annie's long hair until it looked super shiny.

Then they tried out different shades of eye shadow on Annie. And different lip glosses. And different hairstyles.

They also gave her a super-deluxe facial.

"Ummmmm. I feel like I'm at a beauty spa." Annie said.

"Ooh la la. Your skin—I mean your complexion—looks as smooth as velvet now," Nancy said after they wiped the gook off her face.

"I'd better not get a zit before twilight tomorrow!" Annie said just as Bree's parents returned home. "Wish me *bonne chance*." Annie said it like this: "bun shahnss." "That's French for good luck!"

CHAPTER 11

TEENAGERS IN LOVE

On Friday Mr. D brought in cup-
cakes.

Everyone read their Appreciation Hearts.
Nancy got five nices and twelve fancys.

The one Grace made for Nancy said *I
appreciate Nancy because she is not boring.*
Nancy read it a couple of times. Was this

a compliment? Did it mean Grace thought she was interesting?

The most special ones came from Mr. Dudeny and, of course, Bree.

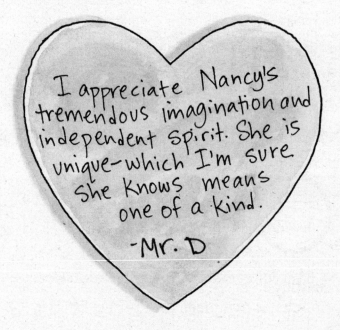

I appreciate Nancy's tremendous imagination and independent spirit. She is unique—which I'm sure she knows means one of a kind.

-Mr. D

After the last bell rang, Clara invited Yoko, Nancy, and Bree to her house. But Nancy explained why they had to decline.

"At twilight Annie and Andy are meeting at the Candy Café."

"We're going to spy on them and watch them fall in love," Bree added.

"Oh, please, can we come too?" Clara begged. Nancy was ready to say yes. But Bree was firm. "Sorry. It'd be too risky with four people. Nancy and I have to stay undercover."

Bree had worked out a minute-by-minute schedule.

4:40 Arrive at Candy Café.

4:41 Go next door to Belle's Fashion Boutique.

4:42 Sneak into alleyway between Belle's and Candy Café. Spy through window.

4:43 Wait for Annie to arrive.

4:45–5:00 Watch Annie and Andy fall in love.

♥ ♥ ♥

At 4:40, right on time, Nancy's mother pulled into the parking lot behind the Candy Café.

"Can Bree and I go over to Belle's?"

Nancy's mom looked ready to say no.

"Please, oh please, Mom!" Nancy said. "It's right next door. It's not even twilight yet."

Nancy's mom relented.

At Belle's, Bree and Nancy didn't even stop to check out the jewelry counter. They went straight to the back entrance and ducked into the alley between the two stores.

The Candy Café window was higher

than they'd expected. They had to stand on their tippy toes. From the party room, Nancy could hear lots of little kids singing "Happy Birthday" to guitar music.

"Andy's gig is over now!" Nancy whispered excitedly.

Sure enough, a minute later Andy sat down at a table in the main room. A waitress took his order.

"Perfect! A table for two!" Bree squealed softly.

Now only one thing was missing.

Annie!

At 4:45 on the dot, she arrived. Annie was wearing everything they'd told her to, and she looked stunning, ravishing, breathtaking!

For a moment Annie glanced around

the room. Then she spotted Andy. Andy spotted Annie. They waved to each other.

"She's sitting down at the table! Bree, we did it. It's all coming true!"

Bree's hand was cupped over her mouth. She was speechless.

"Come on. Let's go in and say hi!" Nancy started tugging Bree by the arm.

Bree looked uncertain. "Ooh, I want to. But won't that give it away?"

"We came with my mom to pick up JoJo and Freddy. Remember? It would be rude not to say hi."

"You're right," Bree said. "But don't let

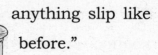

anything slip like before."

At the Candy Café in the party room, JoJo and Freddy and lots of other little kids were racing around tooting party horns. Nancy's mom was sharing a piece of cake with another mom. She saw Nancy and Bree and waved.

At a table in the back, there they were— Annie and Andy. Andy and Annie. They each were holding a spoon. In between them was a banana split. Annie was laughing at something Andy said.

It was like a movie, only better—this was real life!

Bree and Nancy went over and said hi at the same time. It came out too loud.

Andy looked up, startled. Annie swiveled around and said, "Oh! Hi, Bree. Hi, Nancy."

Andy was pointing at the banana split with his spoon. "Want to pull over chairs and help us out? This thing is huge!"

"That's very thoughtful! But we wouldn't dream of disturbing you!" Nancy said.

"You sure?" Andy asked. "We're heading to an all-dessert party later. Gotta leave some room. Right, Annie?"

Ooh la la! Annie and Andy were going to a party. Together! Tonight!

Just then, Nancy caught her mom signaling to them. JoJo and Freddy were in their coats.

"Well, got to go. See you!" Bree grabbed Nancy.

"Wait a sec." Annie stood and, wrapping an arm around Nancy and Bree, steered them to the front of the Candy Café.

"Your secret admirer is my guitar teacher! I can't believe it!" Nancy whispered. "He's tall, dark, and handsome,

just like he told you!"

"And I know for a fact that Andy isn't too nice. I—I mean he's nice, but not yucky nice, like your last boyfriend," Bree babbled excitedly.

"This is meant to be," Nancy went on. "It's love eternal. You already look like you've known each other forever!"

Annie had a funny look on her face.

"That's because we *have* known each other forever."

Bree and Nancy stopped in their tracks. "What do you mean?" they asked Annie.

"Andy and I have been buddies since ninth grade." Annie bit her lip. Then she went on. "And look, you guys. I knew you were behind the whole secret-admirer thing."

"You did? How?" Bree asked. Nancy was too shocked to utter a word.

"The writing." Annie turned to Bree. "I've watched you practice script a lot."

Nancy felt like weeping. She could see Bree did too.

"So why did you play along?" Bree asked.

Nancy was wondering the same thing.

"Because it was so sweet. You want me

to find eternal love. And . . ." Annie giggled. "I was curious to see who you picked out."

Now Nancy felt silly. Annie had been playing along, the way Andy played along with JoJo's "Say please" game. To Annie, Nancy and Bree were just dumb little kids.

Then a terrible thought struck Nancy.

"Does Andy know?" she asked. If he did, she would die; she would perish! She

would have to get another guitar teacher. And she would never play "Wild Thing" again. Ever.

Annie shook her head. "He thinks I just happened to show up here."

That was a relief. But Nancy was still confused. "But—but Andy said you're going to a party together. Isn't that a date?"

Annie shook her head. "Sorry. Andy and I are friends. It's strictly platonic." Then she hugged them both. "You guys are the best."

In the car on the way home, Nancy asked, "Mom, what does platonic mean?"

"Platonic? Hmmm, how can I describe it?" Mom said. "It means that—JoJo, Freddy, that's enough with the horns!" When JoJo and Freddy stopped tooting,

Mom started over. "It means that you like someone as a friend but not in a romantic way."

Nancy and Bree exchanged sad looks. That was what Nancy figured platonic meant. It was the first fancy word she didn't like!

"That's how it started with Dad and me," Mom went on. "We were buddies. I helped him study. Remember? I told you that. Then one weekend we went to a party together. And—I don't know. I guess love was in the air that night."

"Oh! So you went from platonic to romantic?" As Nancy took this in, she and Bree exchanged looks again. Nancy could read Bree's mind. Just like Nancy, she was thinking that maybe this would

happen to Annie and Andy. Maybe it would happen this very night!

After all, it was Valentine's Day. So love was definitely in the air!